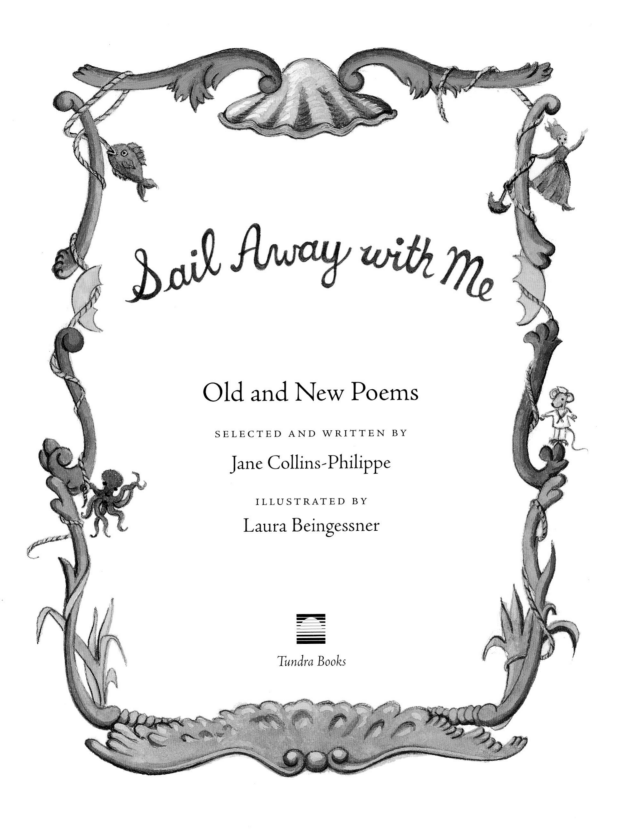

Sail Away with Me

Old and New Poems

SELECTED AND WRITTEN BY

Jane Collins-Philippe

ILLUSTRATED BY

Laura Beingessner

Tundra Books

Published in Canada by Tundra Books,
75 Sherbourne Street, Toronto, Ontario M5A 2P9

Published in the United States by Tundra Books of Northern New York,
P.O. Box 1030, Plattsburgh, New York 12901

Library of Congress Control Number: 2009928988

Library and Archives Canada Cataloguing in Publication

Collins-Philippe, Jane
Sail away with me / Jane Collins-Philippe ; illustrated by
Laura Beingessner.

Poems.
ISBN 978-0-88776-842-2

1. Sea poetry, Canadian (English). 2. Sea poetry. 3. Children's poetry,
Canadian (English). 4. Children's poetry. I. Beingessner, Laura, 1965- II. Title.

PS8605.O471S35 2009   JC811'.6   C2009-902979-0

We acknowledge the financial support of the Government of Canada through the Book
Publishing Industry Development Program (BPIDP) and that of the Government of Ontario
through the Ontario Media Development Corporation's Ontario Book Initiative. We further
acknowledge the support of the Canada Council for the Arts and the
Ontario Arts Council for our publishing program.

The illustrations for this book were rendered in watercolor

Printed and bound in China

1 2 3 4 5 6   15 14 13 12 11 10

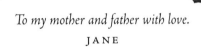

To my mother and father with love.
JANE

To my mother and father,
for their suppoprt and ecnouragement.
LAURA

I Saw a Ship

I saw a ship a-sailing,
A-sailing on the sea,
And oh, but it was laden
With pretty things for thee!

There were comfits in the cabin,
And apples in the hold;
The sails were made of silk,
And the masts were made of gold.

The four-and-twenty sailors,
That stood between the decks,
Were four-and-twenty white mice,
With chains around their necks.

The captain was a duck,
With a packet on his back,
And when the ship began to move,
The captain said, "Quack! Quack!"

– Anon

New Year's Day in the Morning

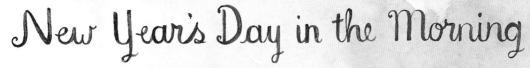

I saw three ships come sailing by,
Come sailing by, come sailing by.
I saw three ships come sailing by,
On New Year's Day in the morning.

And, what do you think was in them then,
Was in them then, was in them then?
And what do you think was in them then,
On New Year's Day in the morning?

Three pretty girls were in them then,
Were in them then, were in them then.
Three pretty girls were in them then,
On New Year's Day in the morning.

One could whistle and one could sing,
And one could play on the violin.
Such joy was there at my wedding,
On New Year's Day in the morning.

– *Anon*

Wynken, Blynken and Nod

Wynken, Blynken and Nod one night
Sailed off in a wooden shoe;
Sailed off on a river of crystal light,
Into a sea of dew.
"Where are you going, and what do you wish?"
The old moon asked the three.

"We have come to fish for the herring fish
That live in the beautiful sea.
Nets of silver and gold have we!"
Said Wynken, Blynken and Nod.

The old moon laughed and sang a song,
As they rocked in the wooden shoe,
And the wind that sped them all night long,
Ruffled the waves of dew.

The little stars were the herring fish
That lived in the beautiful sea;
"Now cast your nets wherever you wish,
Never afeared are we;"
So cried the stars to the fishermen three:
Wynken, Blynken and Nod.

All night long their nets they threw
To the stars in the twinkling foam;
Then down from the skies came the wooden shoe
Bringing the fishermen home;

'Twas all a pretty sail it seemed
As if it could not be,
And some folks thought 'twas a dream they dreamed
Of sailing that beautiful sea.
But I shall name you fishermen three:
Wynken, Blynken and Nod.

Wynken and Bynken are two little eyes,
And Nod is a little head,
And the wooden shoe that sailed the skies
Is the wee one's trundle bed.

So shut your eyes while mother sings
Of wonderful sights that be;
And you shall see beautiful things
As you rock in the misty sea,
Where the old shoe rocked the fishermen three:
Wynken, Blynken and Nod.

– *Eugene Field*

My Bonnie Lies over the Ocean

My Bonnie lies over the ocean;
My Bonnie lies over the sea.
My Bonnie lies over the ocean;
Oh, bring back my Bonnie to me.

Bring back, bring back,
Bring back my Bonnie to me, to me!
Bring back, bring back,
Bring back my Bonnie to me!

Oh blow ye the winds o'er the ocean;
And blow ye the winds o'er the sea.
Oh blow ye the winds o'er the ocean,
And bring back my Bonnie to me.

Bring back, bring back,
Bring back my Bonnie to me, to me!
Bring back, bring back,
Bring back my Bonnie to me!

The winds have blown over the ocean;
The winds have blown over the sea.
The winds have blown over the ocean;
And brought back my Bonnie to me.

Bring back, bring back,
Bring back my Bonnie to me, to me!
Bring back, bring back,
Oh, bring back my Bonnie to me!

– *Anon*

Splish Splash

If all the seas were one sea,
  What a great sea that would be.

If all the trees were one tree,
  What a great tree that would be.

If all the axes were one axe,
  What a great axe that would be.

And if all the men were one man,
  What a great man that would be.

And if the great man took the great axe,
  And cut down the great tree,
  And let it fall into the great sea,
  What a splish-splash that would be!

  – *Anon*

The Owl and the Pussycat

The Owl and the Pussycat went to sea
In a beautiful pea-green boat,
They took some honey, and plenty of money
Wrapped up in a five-pound note.
The Owl looked up to the stars above,
And sang to a small guitar,
"O lovely Pussy! O Pussy my love,
What a beautiful Pussy you are!"

Pussy said to the Owl, "You elegant fowl!
How charmingly sweet you sing!
O let us be married; too long we have tarried:
But what shall we do for a ring?"
They sailed away for a year and a day,
To the land where the bong-tree grows,
And there in a wood a Piggy-wig stood,
With a ring at the end of his nose, his nose,
With a ring at the end of his nose.

"Dear Pig are you willing to sell for one shilling
Your ring?" Said the Piggy, "I will."
So they took it away, and were married next day
By the Turkey who lives on the hill.
They dined on mince, and slices of quince,
Which they ate with a runcible spoon;
And hand in hand, on the edge of the sand,
They danced by the light of the moon, the moon,
They danced by the light of the moon.

– *Edward Lear*

Bobby Shaftoe

Bobby Shaftoe went to sea,
Silver buckles on his knee.
He'll come back and marry me,
Pretty Bobby Shaftoe.

Bobby Shaftoe's fine and fair,
Combing down his auburn hair.
He's my friend forevermore,
Pretty Bobby Shaftoe.

– Anon

Swan Swam

Swan swam over the sea,
Swim, swan, swim!
Swan swam back again,
Well swum, swan!

— *Anon*

A Bug and a Flea

A bug and a flea
Went out to sea,
Upon a reel of cotton.
The bug was drowned,
And the flea was found
Biting a lady's bottom!

— *Anon*

A Little Old Woman

A little old woman, as I have heard tell,
Lived near the sea in a nice little shell;
She was well off if she wanted her tea –
She had plenty of water from out of the sea.

Then, if for her dinner she had the least wish,
Of course, she had nothing to do but fish;
So really, this little old woman did well,
And she didn't pay rent for the use of the shell.

– *Anon*

Finger Fun

One, two, three, four, five –
Once I caught a fish alive.
Six, seven, eight, nine, ten –
Then I let it go again.
Why did I let it go?
Because it bit my finger so.
Which finger did it bite?
The little finger on the right.

– *Anon*

A Boat for Jillian

In a land far away
From you and me
Lives a girl named Jillian Kane.
"With my boat," says she, "I'll go out to play
On the big, blue beautiful sea.

"My boat's *The Pearl*,
She's strong and fine
With her fishing nets
And flags all flying.
We shall leave with the moon
And sail till we find
The other side of the world.

"I will set the sails
To catch the breeze
And *The Pearl* will buck
Like a horse set free.
Her bow will dance
Like a leaf on a tree . . .
And I will sing with the whales.

"Well, the wind will blow,
And the waves will rise,
But far from land
With my sailor's eye,
I will find the place
Where the sea meets the sky,
And that is where I'll go."

In a land far away
From you and me,
Lives a girl named Jillian Kane.
"With my boat," says she. "I'll go out to play
On the big, blue beautiful sea!"

She's a Ship

She's a pretty ship
And that's a fact.
To her fine lines,
I tip my hat.

"That's quite a gal,"
Is what they say,
Watching how her
Bows can sway.

For a ship is a lady,
Believe what I'm saying;
All sailors know that,
When *she* takes *them* sailing!

Seagull

Seagull, please,
Come have a sit,
Beside me on
My merry ship.

And how I wish
You'd sing a tune,
To make me dream
About the moon,
And all her shining, magic beams,
Casting diamonds
On the sea.

The Good Ship Royal

On the good ship *Royal*
There's a curious crew;
Surely the most curious
That I ever knew!

The captain's a hippo,
In a proper cap,
First mate is a jackass,
Now, just fancy that!

Working as lookout
Is Joyce, the giraffe.
Her head hits the spreaders!
It's good for a laugh.

The shiphands are weasels
And penguins and sheep,
Who all end up tangled
In everyone's feet.

Their fingers are useless.
(They haven't got any.)
They fumble the lines,
Of which there are many.

So whenever the *Royal*
Prepares to set sail,
The crew that she has
Cannot help but fail.

The captain starts frowning,
He stamps and he snorts,
Then finally decides
They should never leave port.

Ship-hand

Ship-hand

The
Captain

Ship-hand

Joyce
The Look-out

First
Mate

Cruising

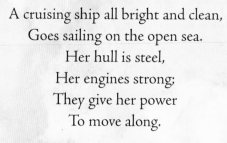

A cruising ship all bright and clean,
Goes sailing on the open sea.
Her hull is steel,
Her engines strong;
They give her power
To move along.

Inside are people
By the hundreds,
Traveling the world from
Wonder to wonder;
To countries small
And countries grand,
They find something special
In every land.

At Home

No matter wherever
She chooses to roam,
The sea will always
Be at home.

When voyaging far,
She won't care a lick,
Wherever she goes,
She's never homesick!

Sea Shell

Finding a shell
Upon a beach,
Is like finding the stone
Inside a peach.

The stone holds the
Peach's life within;
The shell holds the song
Of the sea and the wind.

The sea shell is more,
Than a delicate thing,
In truth, it's the flute
That helps the sea sing.

Something Fishy

I am a fish in the sea.
I'm not sure what's the matter with me.
When I swim upside down,
And can't see the ground,
I get seasick,
As seasick can be!

Salt

Having salt in the sea,
Is like a
Walrus on your knee,
Or a horse up in a tree:
They're funny places
For them to be.

Salty Seas

Sea water is not like water you've seen,
Though that's not anyone's fault.
For whether it's blue or whether it's green,
It's surely going to taste of salt.

People may think it's extremely odd,
But I think it just has to be better,
That the sea is heavily spiced with salt,
Rather than with pepper.

Mary Goes to Sea

Mary went off to sea
In a ship,
But the ship was so small,
There was nowhere
To sit!

So, up the mast
She was told to go,
And if she saw land,
To shout, "Land-ho!"

Now, the mast was thin,
And Mary was not,
So she hung on tight;
Like a double-tied knot.

The boat started to roll,
Then started to rock,
Mary was scared
From her head to her socks.

"May I please come down,
Oh, captain?" she pleaded.
"I'll tend to the lines
And do what is needed."

But the captain was mean,
The captain was cruel.
"Stay where you are," he cried,
"Don't be a fool!"

Just then a huge wave hit;
Poor Mary let go!
She fell from the mast,
To the captain below.

The captain was flattened –
A right chocolate-chip cookie –
But Mary just laughed
And said, "Well, lookie, lookie!"

For, perched as she was
On the captain's poor bean,
She felt rather pleased,
If you know what I mean.

She gathered some ropes
And tied him up tight.
He couldn't get loose –
Try as he might.

And boy, was he angry;
He hollered a lot,
But according to Mary
Deserved what he got.

She hoisted him out
To the end of the boom.
For the rest of the trip
She had plenty of room!

Sailing

A white moon sets our sails alight,
As we follow the sea through an indigo night.
Stars, like eyes, will help us see,
So we don't lose our way on this wide, black sea.

The sun will rise from where we came,
And quietly paint the sea with flame.
Then on we will go like a shimmering pearl
And sail our boat to the end of the world.

Baby's Boat

Baby's boat's the silver moon
Sailing in the sky,
Sailing o'er the sea of sleep,
While the clouds float by.

Sail, baby, sail,
Out upon the sea,
Only don't forget to sail
Back again to me,
Back again to me.

Baby's fishing for a dream,
Fishing near and far,
His line a silver moonbeam is,
His bait a silver star.

Sail, baby, sail,
Out upon the sea,
Only don't forget to sail
Back again to me,
Back again to me.